TO AME
SA...

WITH BEST WISHES.

PETE.

Pete Smith is a pianist by profession. He has worked with top class entertainers and musicians in many cities around the world.
He now resides on the island of Crete with his wife Anne and their adorable furry family.

The Adventures of Harry, Poppy, Dixie & Introducing Alfie

To all those caring people who have rescued and adopted orphaned and stray animals.

Pete Smith

The Adventures of Harry, Poppy, Dixie & Introducing Alfie

Austin Macauley
PUBLISHERS LTD.

Copyright © Pete Smith

The right of Pete Smith to be identified as author of this work has been asserted by him in accordance with section 77 and 78 of the Copyright, Designs and Patents Act 1988.

All rights reserved. No part of this publication may be reproduced, stored in a retrieval system, or transmitted in any form or by any means, electronic, mechanical, photocopying, recording, or otherwise, without the prior permission of the publishers.

Any person who commits any unauthorized act in relation to this publication may be liable to criminal prosecution and civil claims for damages.

A CIP catalogue record for this title is available from the British Library.

ISBN 978 184963 361 1

www.austinmacauley.com

First Published (2013)
Austin Macauley Publishers Ltd.
25 Canada Square
Canary Wharf
London
E14 5LB

Printed and Bound in Great Britain

Acknowledgments

Thank you to my wife Annie for her enthusiasm and encouragement about my story.

To Patti, our dear friend, for her delightful drawings.

To Susan for her dedication in deciphering my handwritten manuscript.

Contents

Prologue — 15

Chapter 1 — 18
In The Beginning

Chapter 2 — 23
Midnight Run

Chapter 3 — 30
A Sad Day

Chapter 4 — 35
Our New Home

Chapter 5 — 41
Bag Of Bones

Chapter 6 — 46
A Bridge Too Far

Chapter 7 — 50
Oh No! Not Another Bridge

Chapter 8 — 55
Three Kittens

Chapter 9 — 62
Where Eagles Dare

Chapter 10 — 70
Red

Chapter 11   **79**
The Great Escape

Chapter 12   **84**
The Colour Of Money

Chapter 13   **89**
A Christmas Story

Epilogue   **98**

Prologue

Bobby Badger was shuffling along, minding his own business on that crisp moonlit night. Suddenly he heard a kind of swish swishing sound above him. Looking up, he could hardly believe his eyes – five eagles in formation! There was no mistaking the leader, Old Ike. So the Feather Gang were back in town with what looked like two new recruits.

Crikey, thought Bobby, I must hurry to warn Harry and the family.

As we strolled out for our final walk of the evening, we bumped into a grim looking Bobby Badger.

"Hello Bobby," I said. "Happy Christmas! But why so glum?"

"Well it's not so 'appy, is it?" he replied. "I've got bad news for you."

"Oh, what's up?" I asked.

"It's Old Ike and the Feather Gang – they're back in town!"

Oh dear, I thought, as I cast my mind back to that dreaded day – a day none of us will ever forget. How brave Alfie was, how courageous Billy was, and how the rest of us were sick with worry.

What on earth were we going to do? Ike and his gang would want revenge, as Alfie and Billy made fools of them, and they would certainly want to get even. They were a ruthless lot and Bobby told me that they had recruited two more members to the gang – the notorious Clanton Brothers – so he sure means business!

I must call the family for a meeting, with Billy and Bobby, and not to forget Old Angus – there's a wise head on those shaggy shoulders – and besides, he owes us a favour. We would have to put our heads together to come up with a plan, and it would have to be a good one to outwit the Feather Gang. If Old Ike wanted a fight, we would have to be very well prepared.

What a start to the new year, I thought. But I'm digressing now, and should take you back to where it all began…

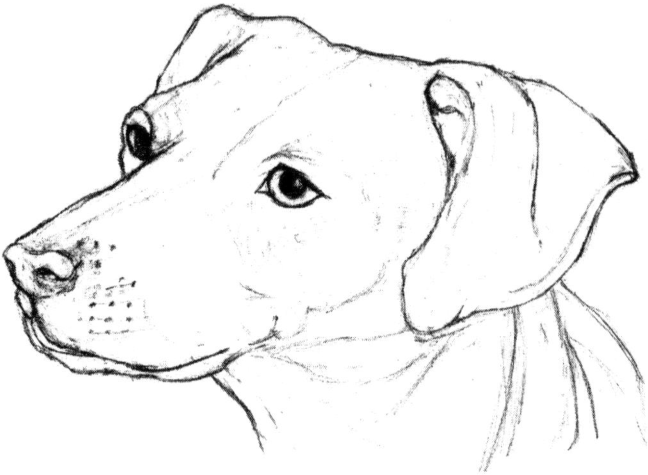

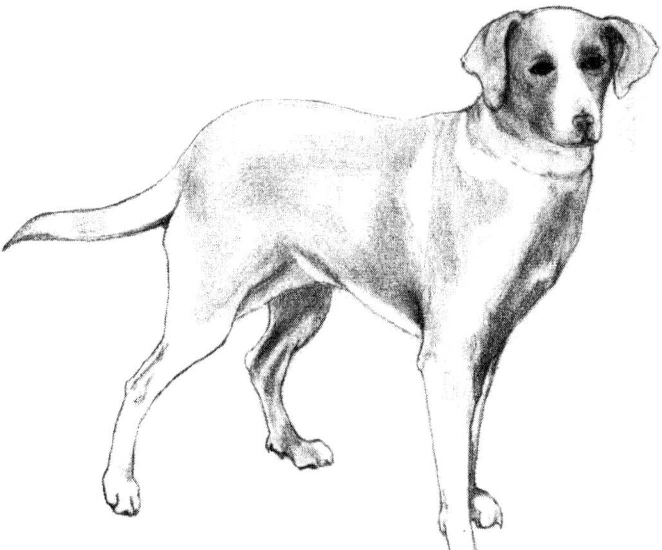

Chapter 1

In The Beginning

Although I have a faint memory of my mother's warm breath on my face, and snuggling up with sister, my first real recollection of puppyhood was the pair of us in the arms of a young man walking down a garden path. There he stopped to talk to an older man and, after some chitchat, I was gently handed over and taken into his house.

After closing the door, he put me down and I looked around, trying to get my bearings. I was shaking like a leaf as I didn't quite know what to expect. I just felt like crying. I was hungry, thirsty and missing my Mum. Where was she? And where did my sister go?

At that moment a soft voice said in my ear, "Don't worry little one – we'll take care of you" and, turning around, there stood a vision! I don't think I will ever forget the first time I saw that adorable face – soft hazel eyes and long silky ears.

"I'm Dixieland," she said. "Dixie for short, or even shorter, just plain Dix. Welcome to our home. You couldn't have chosen better. I have a wonderful Mum and Dad and never want for anything. How old are you? But I don't suppose you know, do you? Very young, I think, and... blah... blah... blah..."

On and on she went, although, somehow it was reassuring and I was starting to feel a little better.

Just then, the same man came in.

"Hello Dixie. How d'yer like your new friend?" he asked, and placed on the floor a bowl of water and a dish of food. After a few kind words and a pat on the head, he left us.

"Eat up," said Dixie. "You'll enjoy that. The food's always good. In fact, life's good being here – I hope you'll stay. You will, won't you?"

"Well, I…"

"I've got lots of friends I'll introduce you to. Then there's the sea and beach at the bottom of the garden, as well as a grassy knoll where Dad takes me all the time. That's where I often meet Stelios and Henry – you'll love them."

"Who are Stelios and Henry?" I asked.

"Stelios is a little Terrier and Henry's a Boxer. Good friends."

"Well, I…"

"Then there's Big Max. You'll see a lot of him, 'cos he fancies me and is always coming round. So, what d'you think?"

"Well, if they want me… I mean, I don't know where I am or where my Mummy is, but, at least I'll be near my sister and… Oh dear…"

"Oh, my beautiful boy, of course they'll want you. Wait till Mum sees you – she's at work now. She'll adore you. And, judging by the size of your paws, you're going to grow big and I think Dad would like a big dog. Oh! And listen – about your Mummy – my Mum and Dad found me on the beach when I was about your age. I was with my six brothers and sisters together with our Mummy. We were all skin and bone, being winter, and there was no one around to feed us. After some debate Dad picked me up and, promising my family that they would find good homes for all of them, we left. Sure enough, some days later I heard Mum say that all the young ones, plus Mummy, had new homes. So have good thoughts. Already your sister is safe with our friends in the next apartment, and who's to say that your Mummy isn't safe as well? So, finish your food, get a good night's sleep and, in the morning, I'll show you around."

At that moment Mum arrived home and, spotting me, clapped her hands and said,

"Oh! What a handsome boy. Where've you come from?"

Dad told her the story of how Andreas, our neighbour, had found the two pups at the side of the road, wrapped in an old T-shirt.

"Shame" she said. "You're all skin and bones aren't you? Never mind – we'll soon get you right, and Dixie will be happy to have a little brother, won't you Dix?"

"You keep him warm in your basket tonight Dixie," said Dad. "I'll get one for him tomorrow, and we'll have to find him a name."

The following morning, Mum and Dad had obviously been discussing it and had reached a decision and I was given the name Harry. Yes, I thought, I'll go along with that – it's got a nice ring to it!

So began my wonderful life with the lovely Dixie, who showed me all the dos and don'ts of family life.

Our Dad worked at night – he played the piano in a hotel – so we had the days together and had many adventures. Our Mum also worked in a hotel, but during the day; she treated people who had sore necks and backs. On her day off we'd all pile into the car and go to a beach – Long Beach it was called – where our Mum and Dad would meet some of their friends. They were quite happy to sunbathe, but we all played games and swam. We'd chase after sticks, although Dixie's favorite game was to try to catch small stones thrown by our Mum and Dad. She'd leap high into the air with all four legs off the ground. Then it was into the sea, and this is where I learnt to swim. At first I wasn't too sure of the water but, once Dad carried me in, my legs just automatically started pumping and I glided along, never seeming to tire. It's been my passion ever since. Dixie enjoyed it too but just for short spells – she was far happier jumping for her stones.

Back at the house, we would go swimming nearly every day, as we were lucky enough to have the sea at the bottom of the garden, as Dixie had told me on that first day. On one of these days, whilst swimming next to our Dad, I noticed a man nearby floating with his head in the water and not moving. Also, there seemed to be a short stick poking out from his head.

That man's in trouble, I thought, and made my way towards him. Dad called me back, but I wanted to see if he needed help. I mean, apart from not moving, what was he doing with a stick poking out of his head? Well, I swam right close to him. Suddenly he shot right out of the water making a sort of 'aaaarghhhh' sound. He scared the daylights out of me and I swam away as fast as my legs would take me. Meantime, the man started shouting at our Dad who seemed to shout back some words of apology. Later, our Dad was in hysterics telling Mum all about it.

"This man," he said -Dad called him a 'snorkeller', a funny name, I thought! – "got such a fright when Harry loomed up in front of him that he leapt right out of the water. He was looking for fish. The last thing he was expecting was a dog!"

Our Mum and Dad cried with laughter. Me? I didn't think it was at all funny. I mean, there I was going out of my way to help someone in his hour of need, as I thought, when he jumps right out of the water, giving me a heck of a fright. Then he starts shouting at me, and Dad starts shouting at me. No – not fair, and certainly not funny.

My one sadness at this time was that I never saw my sister again. The lady downstairs, Vivienne, who already had two other dogs, Mia and Scruffy, said she couldn't cope with a third, but she told our Mum not to worry as she'd gone to a very nice elderly couple with a big house and garden, and that made me feel a little better. Still, it would have been nice to see her one last time to say goodbye.

Chapter 2
Midnight Run

When we were not with our Mum and Dad, our days were spent playing, either in the garden or on the beach with our friends. Of course, we saw a lot of our neighbours Mia and Scruffy. Mia was a beauty with a black shiny coat, a lovely figure and long eyelashes. Wow! Did I fancy her! Unfortunately for me, so did Scruffy! He was quite small with long bushy eyebrows, which kind of reminded me of a friend of Dad's. Like most short dogs, he was arrogant, full of himself and very protective of Mia. Anytime that I went near her he would say, "Watch yourself Harry", or "Keep your distance, Harry." I would just brush past him smiling and say something like, "Mind your manners, Scruffy." Look, him being a little chap, I could have flattened him with one blow, but I just kept him in his place with a few quiet words.

Stelios was another playmate and, of course, Big Max, who was Dixie's suitor. As she had said, he came round often. Now, that was a big dog, but a gentle giant. Everybody loved Max and he loved everybody – especially Dixie. You could see it a mile off, and he got all coy when she spoke to him.

"Hello Maxie," she would say, and he'd get an attack of the stutters when he replied.

"He... he... hello Dixie. N... n... nice to see you," and off they would run with me in tow.

Often Mia, Scruffy and Stelios would join us, and it would be like The Wild Bunch charging down the beach.

One wintry night, Dad had taken us out for one final walk in the garden. It was cold, the rain was pouring down and Dad was anxious to get back inside. Suddenly, a soaking wet Max came walking through the garden gate.

"Hello Max," said Dad. "What are you doing out on a night like this? You should be indoors. Maybe you'd better come inside and get dry. I'll phone Dimitri, your boss, in case he's worried. Come on."

Well we got as far as the veranda, turned round, and... Max and Dixie had disappeared, just like that! One minute they were there, and the next they were gone. Dad called and called, but nothing.

"What's up?" called Mum.

"Dixie has disappeared, she's ran off with Max," answered Dad.

"You're kidding!" said Mum. "In this weather? She'll freeze! You must go and look for them. C'mon! Hurry!"

"Yes, of course," replied Dad. "Come on Harry," he said. "Let's go find them."

Blimey, I thought, in this? It's throwing it down! But call as we might, there was nothing. We searched every which way, calling all the time and, sniff as I might, I could pick up nothing.

We were like drowned rats before Dad said, "C'mon Harry, let's head back. Maybe they've gone home in the meantime."

But they hadn't. Our Mum was beside herself.

"Where can they have got to? She'll die in this weather! It's only three degrees outside. You must find her, and Max!"

"Right," replied Dad. "I'll go out on the bike and look further afield."

"Be careful," said our Mum as he put on his waterproofs and helmet. "In the meantime, I'll phone Dimitri and see if maybe Max took her there."

"Good idea," shouted Dad as he started the bike and, with a roar, he was gone.

By this time, Mum was near to tears. She had phoned, but with no luck. They weren't there.

It was getting late when Dad returned, saying he'd not seen a sign of either dog. It was then that I had an idea. I went and stood by the door, pawing it, and pretending I wanted to go out.

"Oh Harry. You don't really want to go out in this do you?"

Yes I do, I thought, pawing the door again.

"Oh, go on then, but make it quick."

As I bounded down the garden path, I knew exactly where I was going, and this is where the story really begins.

During the past months, one of my favourite walks, although a short one, was to the end of the beach and onto a grassy knoll. It was a stiff climb to the top and good exercise, for both of us and our Dad. Once down again, it would be into the sea for a welcome swim. Very often on this walk, we would meet up with our Boxer friend Henry and his strange master, Joseph, from a far off land. I said strange; well, can you believe it, this was his home! He used the beach chalets to eat, sleep and keep a change of clothes in, although I didn't see him in a change of clothes, nor did I see him eat. What he always had, though, was either a bottle of raki or red wine. Oh, and a book to read. Always reading, he was. He would always offer our Dad a drink, or 'spot' as he called it. But Dad declined, saying that it was bit early for him, and besides, he only drank beer.

Dad tried to get me to drink some beer once, but I don't think I have ever tasted anything so awful. Once he told our Mum about a man and his dog, a Doberman – the dog, not the man – who used to go into the bar where Dad worked as a young man. He said that every Friday the pair would enter the bar and the man would order two pints of lager and two mutton curries – hot! The dog would wolf his curry down and chase it with the beer, which had been put down into his own bowl. Dad said it was good for business, as people came from far and wide to marvel at the curry eating, beer-drinking dog. Dad said that it was a really fiery Indian curry that even most of the locals couldn't handle. Dad tried me on some curry once. But one bite and I dived for my water bowl!

Anyway, where was I? Oh, yes – Joseph! He and Dad used to chat while we played our games. He told Dad that he preferred to live with nature and his dog, Henry. He did odd jobs to keep him in food and drink, although, as I said, I never saw him eat. However, Henry looked healthy enough, and Joseph always had a snack for us. We'd play for hours whilst Joseph and our Dad talked of many things. We were always exhausted by the time we got home, but it was one of our favourite spots.

This, then, was where I headed in the pouring rain, in the freezing cold.

Dixie, I thought, you picked a fine time to go out on a date! I took a shortcut through the grounds of the small hotel next to us, which was closed for the winter and dark and spooky. Dashing onto the beach, I found myself up to my knees in the cold sea as the waves rushed in. Soon the beach widened and pebbles gave way to sand.

I stopped and called out "Dixie! Max!" and, sure enough, there was an answering call from not far away.

"We're here!" shouted Dixie. "We're alright, Harry."

Yeah, nice, I thought. You're alright, but what about me? I was freezing cold and soaking wet, but I was relieved to hear her voice and know she was safe.

Henry, Max and Dixie came out from one of the beach huts to meet me, followed by Joseph.

"Hello, Harry," he said. "Dixie and Max came from the beach drenched and shivering, so I thought it best to keep them here till the rain eased off."

Yeah, great!, I thought. You tell that to our Mum. She'll box your ears!

"C'mon Dix," I urged, "we'd best get going. Your Mum's frantic. Whatever possessed you to go gallivanting off in this weather?"

"I'm sorry," she replied, "but Max said he had something to show me and..."

"And you fell for that old line? What are you like?"

I turned and glared at Max. "I'll talk to you later! Meantime, you'd better come with us back to the house. C'mon." And, bidding goodbye to Henry and Joseph, we ran as fast as we could in the rain and the dark, along the beach, through the hotel grounds and up the garden path to the front door.

"Oh, thank goodness," sobbed Mum, opening the door.

"Cor," said Dad, "I see you found them, Harry. Good boy. Well done! I'd just about given you all up. Do you know it's after midnight, Max? What do you mean by running off with Dixie?"

He looked at Max sternly and continued. "You should know better – a dog your age! Anyway, let's get you all dry. Max, I'll phone your boss, Dimitri. He will be worried sick. I'll tell him to pick you up in the morning. Now, all of you, have a quick bite and get to bed."

And that's what we did, but just before I nodded off, I turned to Dixie and said, "Next time you go on a date, Dix, please try and pick a warm and moonlit night!"

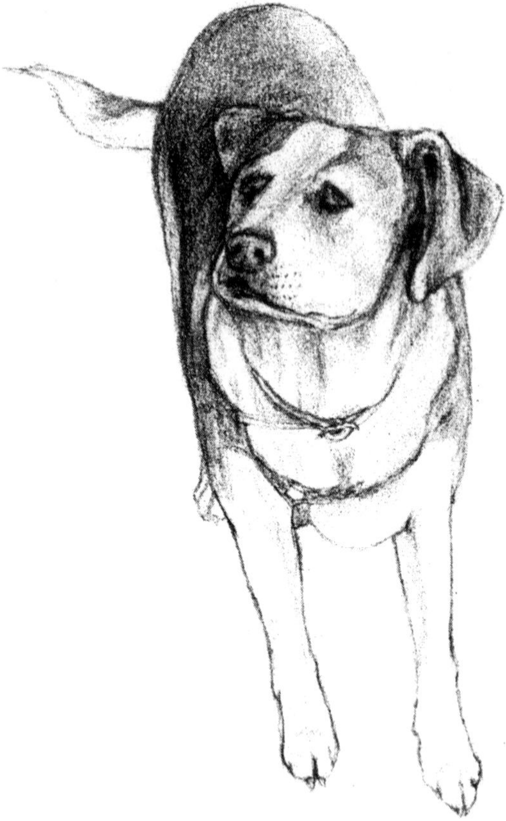

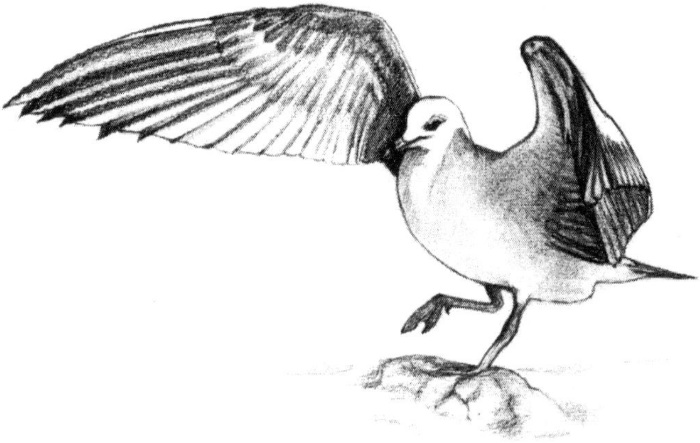

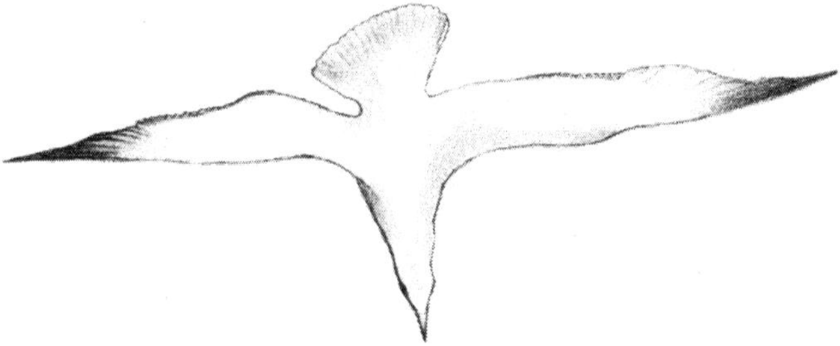

Chapter 3

A Sad Day

The following morning Max's boss came round to fetch him. He brought Dad a nice bottle of wine to thank him for looking after Max – nice, that. Max was so pleased to see Dimitri that he almost wagged his tail off!

"He loves you so much," said Dad. "You wouldn't think that he'd wander off, yet I see him all over the place."

"I know," replied Dimitri. "He's a free spirit. Loves to visit all his friends – especially Dixie, it seems. I try to keep him at home, but he's got a mind of his own. The road worries me, but what can I do?"

"Well, if he disappears again, you'll know where to look. He's found himself a girlfriend," Dad laughed.

Max did come visiting often, but I gave him a hairy eye, which said 'Don't even think about it' and he got the message, but we were all good friends.

We had a lot of fun and were often joined by Mia and Scruffy. One fine day on the beach, a large gull fell from the sky at an amazing speed, pulled out of the dive just above the sand, and screeched to a halt in front of us.

"Hiya fellas," he said. "Having fun?"

"Wow," said Scruffy. "That's some flying! And yes, we are having fun. Want to join us?"

"That would be nice," the gull answered. "I'm not much for running around, but I can teach you a new game of tag, and I'm a good swimmer."

"That'll be good," said Dixie. "It'll be nice to have a new playmate. Let's introduce ourselves." And she rattled off all our names.

"Great to meet you all," said the bird. "I'm Jonathan Livingston Seagull."

"Do what?" grinned Scruffy.

"That's a mouthful," said Mia. "Where did you get a name like that?"

"Rather aristocratic, isn't it?" said the seagull. "And I'm very proud of it. In my youth, I held the air speed record for gulls."

"Wow!" said Mia. "How fast did you go?"

"Over two hundred miles an hour. But that wasn't all – I was also the ace of aerobatics."

"You're kidding?" I cried. "So you must be the *famous* Jonathan Livingston Seagull. I've heard our Dad talk of you. Well, we're honoured to meet you, and I'm sure the gang would love to see your tricks. Would you do that for us?"

"Well," he said, "I'm a bit rusty, and not as young as I used to be, but here goes."

With that, he took off and climbed high in the sky. When he was a mere dot, he stopped, turned and came screeching down; then he did an assortment of twists, turns and rolls like I've never seen. We all cheered as, with one final dive, he pulled out inches above the sea, skimmed across the waves at a tremendous speed, skidded to a halt and took a bow.

"Wow!" said Dix. "If that was you old and rusty, what were you like in your heyday?"

"I was pretty good" he replied. "But enough of me. Let's have some fun. Oh and, by the way, just call me Jon!"

Jon was to join us on many a romp on the beach and would always end with us all splashing around in the sea. These were good times. But, as so often happens in life, our world came crashing down. It happened one morning when

Dixie had taken herself out and I was having high jinx with our Dad. I suddenly heard Dixie's cry.

"Harry, come quickly! Something's happened to me!"

I ran out and saw her standing stock still with a look of panic on her face.

"What's the matter, Dix?" I asked.

"I can't see! I can't see! Oh, Harry! Help me!"

"Of course. Now don't panic. Just lean on me and I'll guide you back inside. Dad'll know what to do. I'm sure it's not serious."

But it was. Our Dad got the doctor in but the news was bad. Dixie had a disease of the eyes and wouldn't see again. He gave her drops to soothe them but that was all he could do. We were heartbroken. Dix cried for hours, and it was some days before she could be tempted outside.

"Dix," I said, "it's going to be very hard on you but you've got the best Mum and Dad in the world. They'll look after you, and from now on I'll be your eyes."

Our Dad attached a small bell to my collar so that Dixie could always follow the sound and so know where I was. That was a good idea, wasn't it?

"Stick close to me Dix," I said, "and always listen for the bell."

Dixie was very brave and, as the days passed, she became more and more confident. Of course there were no more high-speed romps for her, but we all understood her plight and did our best to see that she joined in our fun and games. She was amazing – on our walks she kept up a good pace, and on the beach she would run with the rest of us, sensing that there were wide-open spaces with no danger.

One day I said to her, "Dix, how do you do it? You run around as if you can see!"

"Yes," she answered. "I seem to have developed a far better sense of smell. It's as if my angels are helping me."

And that wasn't all of it. Her hearing became so acute that she could detect sounds long before any of us. Even our

Dad's motorbike or Mum's car she'd hear long before it arrived home. Actually, I was quite jealous. I mean, it used to be me that would hear them and jump shouting, "They're home!", but now I was a mile behind Dix. Yes, we were all very proud of our brave little Dixie.

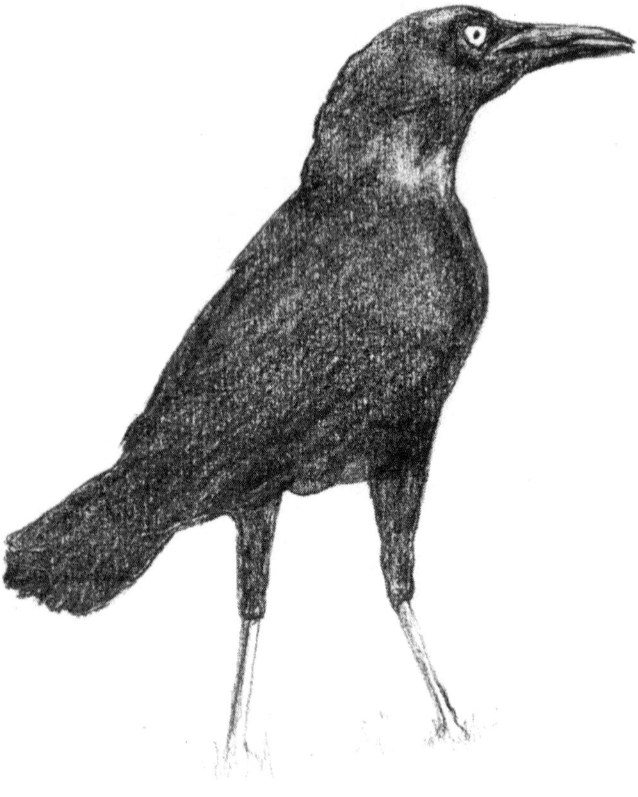

Chapter 4

Our New Home

One day there was great excitement in the household – we were moving to our new home!

It was a long way from here and high in the mountains. We'd been taken to see the progress and it was paradise – wide-open spaces with hundreds of trees and the sea not far away. It had taken two years to complete and, finally, the day had come. The moving van came early in the morning, and by midday it was piled high with our furniture and ready to go. All our friends came to see us off. There was Henry the Boxer, Stelios, Max and, of course, our neighbours, Mia and Scruffy. Even Johnny the gull flew in.

"I'll miss you guys," he said, "but I'll come and visit you."

"That would be nice," answered Dixie. "But you don't know where it is."

"Oh, don't you worry about that," he grinned. "I'll find you. Good luck, guys." And off he flew.

There were a few tears as we said our goodbyes with the promise to visit from time to time. So it was time to go, and with a lurch and cloud of smoke, off went the van with us following in Dad's car.

"Oh my Lord," he said, "I hope it arrives in one piece!"

Mm, I thought, I wouldn't put money on it!

After what seemed many miles, we overtook the van to show them the way and were relieved to see that all was in order. Well, put it this way, we hadn't seen bits and pieces lying in the road! As we reached the small village of Sfaka, you could sense the excitement in the car. Dixie's tail was wagging furiously.

"We're here! We're here!" she shouted.

"How do you know we are here?" I asked, astonished.

"Oh, I know," she grinned.

Amazing! As the car stopped in the drive, Dixie and I leapt out and immediately started exploring.

"Don't go far," shouted Dad. "This is all new to you and I don't want you getting lost!"

Don't worry Dad, I thought. With my eyes and Dixie's nose, there's no chance of that!

"Careful, Dix," I said. "There's plenty of pitfalls around, so stick close to me. Listen for my bell."

I had noticed a very large hole at one end of the garden and at one end there were steps reaching down to the bottom. Very strange, I thought. What on earth is that for? We were to find the answer next day.

That morning after our walk, Dad started filling the hole with water. Now what?, I thought. When the hole was filled to the brim, it all became clear. Our Mum and Dad, wearing a minimum of clothing, walked down the steps into the water and submerged.

Yay, I thought, a swimming hole! It looked great for a hot day, but sadly Dad told us to stay out as it had stuff in it that wasn't good for our coats.

"But don't worry," he said. "I'll be taking you to the sea as often as I can."

Well, I knew the sea was nearby and wondered why anyone would need a funny little hole filled with water that had some stuff in it when there was a great big sea down the road with NO stuff in it. Very weird!

Anyway, beyond the hole there was an area of dense bush that looked inviting.

"C'mon Dix! This way looks fun, but stay close and listen for my bell."

We ran around for what seemed hours, but apart from some friendly sparrows, there was not another soul. That is, until we were confronted by three crows.

"Hi," said one. "Just moved in, 'ave yer?"

"Yes," I said. "How did you know?"

"Watched yer coming, we did. Nice place. Watched it being built, we did."

"Yes, it's lovely," said Dixie. "It's nice to meet you. I do hope we'll be friends. I'm Dixie, and this is Harry."

"Good to see yer," answered the crow. "I'm Russell, and these are my two cousins, Martin and Jeff."

"Russell Cr...!"

"Yes, yes," said he, interrupting. "I know, I know. He was my mum's favourite... Saw all his films, she did, at the open-air movie house... Sat on the wall, she did. So when I came along..."

"Yes," I said, "I get the point. So anyway, what can you tell us about the neighbourhood?"

"Well," Russell replied. "It's pretty friendly, apart from a bunch of eagles. Nasty things, eagles!"

Thinking about it, I said, "Yes, now that you mention it, I did see three or four of them watching us from above."

"That'd be the Feather Gang," he pointed out. Martin and Jeff nodded.

"The what?" I exclaimed.

"The Feather Gang," he answered. "Old Ike and his two sons. A wild bunch, them. Only got one eye, has old Ike. Lost it when he picked on the wrong fella."

"Oh?" asked Dixie. "And who was that?"

"Young Spikey the hedgehog," laughed Russell. "Nice lad. Lives with his parents, the Quills, in your garden. You're bound to bump into them. Oops! I mean, meet them. You don't want to bump into them. You'll end up like Old Ike," he chuckled. "Anyway, we must be off; it's getting dark. Good to meet you. See you around." And off they flew.

Making a mental note about the Feather Gang, I said, "C'mon Dix, time to go. I'm getting hungry."

"You're always hungry," replied Dix as we headed for home. "When it comes to food, you've got perfect pitch!"

By the time we got back, Mum and Dad had a lot of the furniture in place and the pair of them were sitting down, having a breather.

"Hello you two," Mum said as we came in. "Had fun? C'mon, let's eat – you must be starving. I know we are. Then I think we'll have an early night. I'm exhausted. Tomorrow's another day."

That night I don't remember my head touching the basket.

During the building of the house, our Mum and Dad had struck up a friendship with Fred, who lived in the village with his wife, Doris. Fred was good with his hands – so good, in fact, that he had renovated the house they now lived in. Dad had approached him about landscaping the garden and other work that Dad could not manage. They had made a deal, and so now we saw a lot of him. He was a very jolly and friendly man who never failed to bring us dogs a snack whenever he came round. Dixie was always first to hear his car coming and made sure she was first in line for a biscuit. Sadly, Fred's Alsatian dog Sam had died not long ago, and I somehow felt that coming round and making a fuss of us helped him through his sadness. He and Doris came round to dinner a few times, and we looked forward to these visits for they were full of fun. The four of them would laugh for hours. Our Mum always said that Dad was a funny man, but I guess Fred came a close second. But one thing intrigued Dixie and I – half the time we couldn't understand what he was saying! Well, to begin with, anyway, although we sort of worked it out as time passed by.

Look, here's an example. Soon after we moved in, he came round and we ran to meet him.

"Wotcha Dix! Wotcha 'Arry! What's up, eh? Look, I fetched yer rarned some grub,", which roughly meant "Hello Dixie! Hello Harry! How are you? Here, I've brought you some biscuits." See what I mean?

We ran out to greet Fred one day and, jumping out of his car, he said "'Allo Dix! 'Allo 'Arry!"

Well, our Mum was standing nearby and said, "No, Fred! It's not 'Arry – it's Harry with an aitch! Harry!"

So you know what? 'Aitch' became another name by which our Dad often calls me. Three years down the line, Fred still calls me 'Arry!

Summer was over, and both our Mum and Dad had finished work as their respective hotels closed for the winter. These were lovely times for us, as we were with them both day and night. As the days grew shorter and the weather got colder, we had especially blissful evenings.

Dad would say, "Right, let's batten down the hatches", and we'd all enjoy each other's company in the warmth of our home.

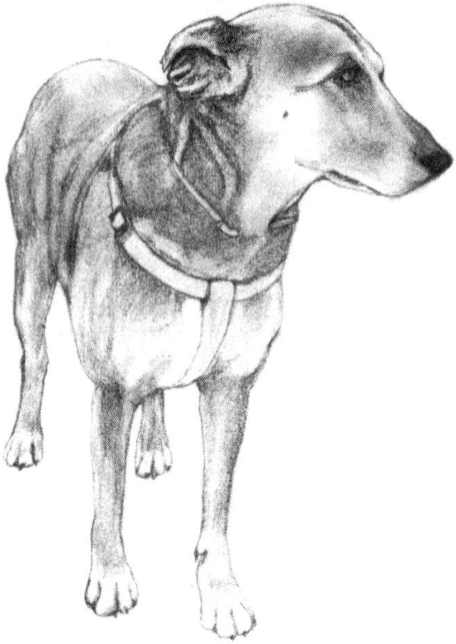

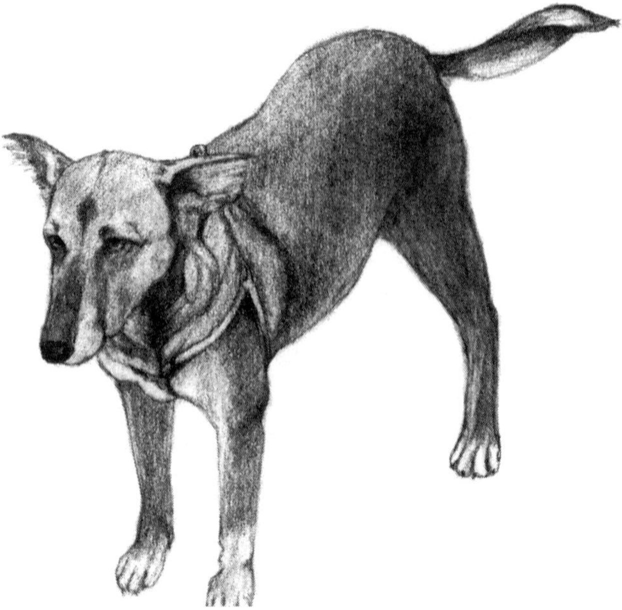

Chapter 5

Bag Of Bones

Once a week, on Wednesday, Mum would spend the day in town to shop and have a chinwag with all her old friends. On one particular Wednesday after we'd got back from our walk with Dad, the phone rang, and I could see by Dad's face that something was up. After replacing the phone, he explained.

"Oh dear! Your Mum's seen a poor little dog, all skin and bones she says, tied up by the side of the road, miles from anywhere. She says that if it's still there on her way back, she's going to rescue it and bring it home."

Blimey, I thought. Not another one to look after – I've enough on my plate with Dixie! Later in the afternoon, Mum again phoned to say she had the dog and would be home presently.

On hearing her arriving, Dad told us to stay inside as he didn't know how the new arrival would react.

"I wonder if it's a boy or a girl?" asked Dixie.

"We'll soon find out 'cos here they come," I replied.

Dad came into view, followed by this scrawny thing, which he had on a chain.

"A girl!" I said with glee.

"Oh, really?" Dixie said, coolly.

"Sit tight, you two," Dad called as he opened the door and released the bag of bones. And do you know what? Without so much as a hello or goodbye, this cheeky mutt ran into the lounge and plonked herself on the sofa!

That's nice!, I thought. Don't mind us – just make yourself at home! Being a girl, I thought this could be fun or it could be trouble and, judging by first impressions, trouble it would be. Better get on top of this, I thought.

So, strolling up to her, I went eyeball to eyeball and said, "Now look, girl! Let's not get off to a bad start. I'll explain a few dos and don'ts and we'll get along fine. Firstly, we don't jump on the sofa without permission. Secondly, when and *if* we do get permission, we certainly don't go in Dad's place. And that's Dad's place, so get down!"

She gave me a sheepish look before jumping to the floor, where she sat looking up at me.

"Right," I said. "By the look of it, you haven't eaten in days, so we'll have some dinner and then talk some more. C'mon."

Our Mum put down our bowls of food with an extra one for Bones. She wolfed it down in seconds, then licked the bowl all round the room. Boy, was she hungry!

When we were finished I took her outside and said, "Listen. Okay, so you were very hungry so I'll forgive your bad manners this time, but in future, when the food's put down, you sit and wait until either our Mum or Dad give you a kiss on the head. Then you eat. Okay?

"So, let's introduce ourselves. That's Dixie and I'm Harry."

"Harry, is it?" she said. "I thought I heard your Dad call you another name – in fact, TWO other names."

"You're right," I replied. "Big Dog and Aitch."

"Aitch," she laughed. "What kind of name is that?"

"Don't go there," I answered. "As far as you're concerned, I'm Harry!"

"What's your name?" joined in Dixie.

Before she could answer, I stared at her, noticing there was something odd about her ears. The tops were missing so that they were square rather than pointed.

"What on earth happened to your ears?" I asked.

"Don't ask," she answered. "It's a sore point. Eh, no pun intended," she added, grinning, and then seriously, "I go cold thinking about that dreadful day. It was my first real memory of puppyhood. I had two brothers and a sister and, one by one, we were held while this horrible man cropped our ears. You can't imagine the pain! I just can't understand why he did it. Anyway, the pain gradually eased, but I got a bit fed up with people pointing at me as if I were a freak or something, especially children. 'Look Mum!' they'd say, pointing. 'Look Mum! Mum! Mum! Look! That dog Mum! He's got funny ears. Mum! Look Mum!' 'Shush now,' the Mums would say. 'It's rude to point!' 'Yes, but Mum…', and so on and so on. Now I actually don't mind. In fact, it's rather nice to be noticed."

"Ooof!" I said, shuddering. "Not a nice story. But tell me, do you have a name?"

"Well, yes I think so," she replied. "You see, it's funny, but the thing is, we all had the same name – Ela!"

"That is funny," said Dixie.

"That's not funny," I said, "and I'll tell you why. That's not a name – it's a Greek word, silly!"

"Not my name? But…"

"That's not your name. No! You hear it all the time. Ela this and ela that. It means come here, go there, start, stop – many things."

"So I don't have a name?"

"So you don't have a name. No."

"Oh dear!" she said. "But…"

"Never mind," I said. "We'll sort it out later. Carry on with the story."

"Yes, right," she replied. "Where was I? Oh yes – we always went out with him together; that is, when we weren't tied up. And that's when the trouble started."

"Trouble?" Dixie said. "What kind of trouble?"

"Well, you see, he used to take us into the hills and he had this big gun that made a loud bang. I hated it. And he used to shoot these poor little birds, and sometimes rabbits, and then tell us to go fetch. I just couldn't do it, and I'd run and hide. My brothers and sister seemed to be okay with it. But me? I just couldn't."

"Yes, I agree," I said. "Terrible! What happened?"

"Well, we went out several times, but I had the same reaction. So, one day he just grabbed hold of me, took me to the car, drove for a bit, got out, tied me to a tree and took off!"

"Which is where our Mum found you," said Dixie, transfixed.

"Exactly," she replied. "Well after some days…"

"Some days? You mean nobody rescued you all that time? I can't believe it! Phew! That's quite a story!"

"But enough of me," she said. "Tell me about yourselves and this place."

I gave her all the details of how we were both rescued, how Dixie lost her sight and of all the friends we left behind when we moved here. She listened attentively and then asked, "Is there much life around here?"

"Well," I replied, "you see the occasional cat and rabbit. Then there are lots of birds and…"

"No, no, no," Bones groaned. "Talent! Males! Some handsome boy that might want to look after a lady!"

"Nothing I'd want to bring home to mother," I replied. "There's a pack that live at the top of that hill yonder, but they're rough – hooligans – so stay away from that lot. For now, you can consider me your knight in shining armour. Now, let's go inside. I expect our Mum and Dad will want to see how you are getting along."

Sure enough, on seeing her they made a big fuss of her and had obviously been talking about her as they had decided on a name for her.

"We shall call you Poppy," said our Mum.

Yes, I thought, that fits. Better than Bones, anyway.

"We've got a spare basket," added our Dad. "Because you'll probably feel a bit lost, you'll sleep with the others in our room, but just for tonight. In future, your place will be in the lounge."

A good idea, I thought, although that arrangement wasn't to last.

The following morning after breakfast we took Poppy out and showed her the neighbourhood.

"We have the run of the land," I explained. "But Dad doesn't like us going up the drive without him near the big road. It's so busy with traffic, and Dad says some days it's like a racetrack. They go so fast. So stay away for your own sake. It's dangerous!"

Later, Dad took us all through the olive groves but kept Poppy on a leash in case she got spooked by something and ran away. As it was, she seemed quite happy walking by Dad's side.

The next few days were spent exploring and she soon got the lay of the land and settled in her new dwelling – except for one thing! She didn't like sleeping on her own in the lounge. I must admit I could understand that. I mean, we were all together during the day and she must have thought that it was some kind of punishment to be shut up on her own. At night she'd wake us up crying in the middle of the night outside the bedroom door. Dad would patiently get up and put her back in her basket with soothing words. But she'd soon be back, crying.

Come on Dad, I thought, let her in. And sure enough, more for the sake of peace than anything else I suspect, the next night our Mum and Dad relented and brought her basket in with ours, and we became one big happy family.

Chapter 6

A Bridge Too Far

"I'm going to do some exploring today," said Dad one morning. "There's an interesting track yonder and I'd like to see where it leads."

"Well don't get lost," said Mum, "and be careful. I wouldn't want to send a search party out for you lot." She grinned.

"Lost?" Dad retorted. "I don't think I could come to much harm around here."

Oh, I don't know about that, I thought. I'd experienced some of his adventures before and, believe me, he's not cut out to be an explorer.

"Well, just watch out," Mum added. "And before you go, check the pump room for the rat you told me about."

"Oh Lord," he said. "I'd forgotten about that. Come with me, Harry, and we'll take a look."

Oh blimey, I thought, I hate rats!

"Dixie," I called. "You come too – you've got a better nose than me." Looking around, I noticed Poppy walking away.

"Where are you going, Pops?" I called.

"Well, I don't like rats either, so I thought I'd take a look around."

"Well, don't be long. As soon as we're finished, Dad's taking us in the car."

"Okay," she said, trotting off.

In the pump room, Dixie sniffed around and said there had definitely been a rat in there, but we didn't see one. Dad messed around with the pool's filter for a while, and then we left.

"Right," said Dad. "Let's get going. Where's Poppy?"

I spotted her coming out of the undergrowth, coming towards us with a strange look on her face. She didn't seem to be walking too well either.

"What's wrong, Pops?" I called.

"Oh dear. My word! I think I'm going to faint!"

"What is it?" I asked. "Are you sick or something?"

"You're not going to believe this," she said, "but I've just met Russell Crowe!"

"Don't be daft" I grinned. "He isn't *the* Russell Crowe! He's Russell *the* crow!"

"Are you sure, Harry?" she asked.

"Course I'm sure, you dummy!"

"Oh dear! And I was going to ask for his autograph," she sighed.

"And what would you do with that?" I laughed. "Come on, Dad is waiting for us."

We all jumped in the car and off we went.

"Right," said Dad. "Let's see where this takes us."

Oh, Dad, I thought, do you think this is a good idea?

As I said earlier, I'd been with him before on his so-called explorations. Take the last adventure, for instance. It took us two hours to get to our destination and four to come back.

We went somewhere on the south coast for the day where we all had a swim and some ball games and afterwards, lunch. Then we took in some sun before our Dad said it was time to go. He first consulted his map and decided that he could take a short cut. It started out alright until I spotted a bridge that I was sure we'd crossed some time back.

"Didn't we cross that bridge some time back, darling?" asked Mum.

"Mm," was all that Dad said, taking a left.

We then entered a small village that I just knew we'd been through before. One or two people gave us a curious look and Mum said, "We've been through here before – I recognise that church!"

"You sure he knows where he's going?" enquired Pops.

"What's happening?" asked Dixie. "Are we lost?"

"You could say that," I replied and added, "This could get interesting."

Then Dad stopped the car, took another look at the map, got under way again, took a couple of turns and... yes! You guessed it! We were back in the village again!

"This is silly," cried Dad. "How'd that happen?"

Glancing out of the window, I noticed that there were a lot more people on the street, some pointing and some even laughing.

"Now I know we're lost," piped Poppy.

"Oh dear," groaned Dixie. "What'll become of us?"

"Don't worry Dixie," I assured her. "We've been through this type of situation before and no doubt we'll go through it again. Our Dad'll get us home... eventually!"

Dad consulted the map again and then set off slowly, glancing this way and that until, "Ah, there we are. This is it", and took a left down a shady lane.

"I really don't think..." started Poppy.

"Shh," I said. "Have some confidence."

Down the shady lane we went, through an olive grove, past a farmyard, over a bridge... Oh no, the same dreaded bridge, and back into the village!

By now the streets were lined with people waving and cheering, and some even had picnics.

"Darling," Mum started. "Don't you think you'd better ask someone?"

Good heavens, I thought. It doesn't take rocket science to figure that one out! I'd have done that on the second circuit. Anyway, that's what he did – stopped the car and explained our dilemma.

"Yes," said the man, "it is a bit confusing. Come, follow me."

And after what seemed like a perfectly straightforward route, he led us to the highway and pointed west. Waving thank you, we headed for home, and thankfully there were no more hiccups.

"Phew," exclaimed Pops as the house came into view. "I began to wonder if I'd ever see this place again."

Now you can see why I was a little concerned over today's outing. I mean, on that last trip, at least Dad thought he knew where he was going, but today it was into the unknown. That was worrying! See what I mean? Anyway, to continue…

Chapter 7

Oh No! Not Another Bridge

After waving goodbye to our Mum, off we went. It was very pleasant at first, winding down the track that was thick with olive trees on either side. The sun was shining, I had a window down and it was glorious with the breeze blowing in my face. Just then, our friend Russell the crow flew by.

"Hello, you guys. Where you off to?" he asked.

"Our Dad's taking us exploring," I explained.

"Exploring?" he said. "There's not much to explore down that way."

"Well," added Poppy, "you try telling that to our Dad – he's the one driving!"

Russell laughed. "Okay," he said. "Have a nice day and take care." And off he flew.

Turning the next bend, I had a sense of doom as we approached a small bridge.

"Oh crumbs," said Poppy. "Not a bridge! You remember the last bridge we met, Aitch?"

"Yes, I do," I replied, "and I don't think it's a good omen."

And I was right! Gradually it got less comfortable as potholes appeared and we were being bumped all over the place. The track started to narrow, overhanging branches hit the roof of the car and the undergrowth grew thicker.

Oh, dear, I thought, we're gonna get lost again! I barked a couple of times but Dad just told me to shush, although I could see by the look on his face that he was a little concerned.

"When's he going to stop?" asked Dixie.

"Yeah – and how's he going to turn around?" added Poppy.

"You took the words right out of my mouth," I said.

We were going at a crawl now as Dad said, "I have to find a place to turn round."

Well, yes, that would help, I thought and, as if by magic a small gap appeared on our left.

"That's it!" cried Dad and turned sharply, but it was a lot steeper than he thought and covered in pine needles.

"He's mad!" cried Pops.

"Not half as mad as Mum'll be if he smashes up the car," added Dixie.

Well, Dad turned the car every which way, but it was clear we weren't going anywhere – we were stuck!

"We're stuck!" Dad said.

Well, that was what I had just said.

"I'll have to leg it back and get help," he explained. "Harry, you watch the car and look after the girls. I'll be as quick as I can."

So off he went and this is where the story really begins.

It was one thing to watch the car, but quite another to watch the car *and* take care of the two girls. Dad hadn't been gone ten minutes when I realised that Poppy was no longer with us. I ran all over the place calling, but nothing.

Oh well, I thought, she is a hunting dog after all, so she'll find her way. Still I worried.

Getting back to the car, Dixie had disappeared.

Oh no! I groaned. This was too much for the brain! Where had she gone? Just then, I heard her calling for help.

"Where are you, Dix?" I shouted.

"I'm down here, you big oaf," she yelled.

I looked over the edge of the bank and spotted her a good two metres down, lying on her back, her legs in the air.

"What are you doing down there?" I called.

"I'm not doing anything down here, you big lump!" she replied. "I fell down here! Now get me up!"

I leapt down as quick as a flash and, gently nudging her, we made it to the top.

"You alright, Dix?" I asked.

"Of course I'm not alright!" she replied angrily. "I'm sore all over and I smell like a polecat!"

It was then that I noticed how close the car was to the edge of the bank.

"Gosh!" I said to Dix. "Another half a metre and we'd all have been wearing wings."

"Wow!" replied Dix. "That close, eh?"

I did a double take in horror before shouting, "It wasn't that close – the car's moved! It's sliding on the pine needles!"

"Oh no!" cried Dixie. "What'll we do?"

"You're not doing anything," I told her. "Just sit tight – I've an idea," and running around, I started pushing rocks under the wheels.

But it wasn't working, and the car slowly slid nearer and nearer to the edge. I yelled, "Dix, don't move! I'm off to find our Dad – he's got to get a move on!"

I was just about to charge off when, thankfully, Fred's banger came chugging round the corner.

"Cor, love a duck!" he shouted through the window. "That's a funny place to park!" And out he jumped, together with our Dad and... Poppy!

"Pops!" I shouted angrily. "Where've you been, and what do you mean by running off like that? A fat lot of good you've been to us."

"A fat lot of good! A fat lot of good! Who d'you think spotted the car sliding towards the edge? And who d'you think sprinted back to hurry up the troops? I did! ME! So don't you 'fat lot of good' me!"

"Now, now, children," said Dixie. "There is still a lot to be done, so let's stop squabbling. We're not out of the woods yet."

But looking around, the big boys seemed to have things under control. Fred had produced a thick rope and attached an end to each car with a lot of huffing and puffing and few choice words thrown in. We all watched, wide-eyed, as he slowly towed our car back on the track. We all let out a sigh of relief as we jumped in.

"How are you going to turn around?" Dad asked Fred.

"Well, I'm not gonna do what you lot did," he laughed. "No, it'll be alright. I'll reverse until I find a track that I can back into." And that's exactly what he did. We all cheered as we made our way home.

"Sorry I shouted at you, Pops," I said, "but I was worried."

"That's alright, Aitch," she answered. "I understand, and all's well that ends well."

"It's not quite ended yet, has it?" joined in Dixie. "I mean, it'll be interesting to see what kind of reception Dad gets from our Mum."

Sure enough, arriving home, there she stood and the body language said it all! With clenched teeth and hands on hips, she wasn't a happy bunny.

"You've been gone for ages! What on earth happened?"

"I know," said Dad. "I'll tell you later. Right now I could murder a beer."

Mum glared at him. "I'll murder you if you don't get those dogs cleaned up! Look at the state of them and smelling like I don't know what!"

A polecat, perhaps? I thought.

"They're not coming in the house like that!"

Oh Lord, I thought, under the hose again and soap in my eyes!

But it was a good way to cool down, and after we were dried off, our Mum, Dad and Fred sat down to their promised beer, whilst us dogs murdered several litres of water.

Chapter 8

Three Kittens

Our Mum and Dad took us on many different walks and seldom missed a day. If the weather was nice, we'd go to our nearby beach, even if it were winter. We'd have our fun and games in the sand, and then, leaving Pops and Dixie running around, Dad and I would go for a long swim.

Dad's friends couldn't believe how he could swim in the winter and, shaking their heads, would say, "You're mad!"

He'd just smile and say, "Probably."

Other times we'd go through the olive groves. There were tracks going every which way so we'd have a choice of routes. Perhaps our favourite one was past a load of beehives – noisy things, these. Then onto a kind of junkyard where there were several cars in various states of repair. This was where one of Dad's friends, Matt, ran a business. They'd become mates when Dad had contrived to trash the car and he'd taken it to Matt to repair.

I actually consider myself lucky to be alive, as Dixie and I were in the car when Dad got out and forgot to put on the handbrake. If the wheels had been pointing right and not left, we'd both be angels! As it was, we watched in horror as the car rolled toward the mountain with Dad running alongside, trying to stop it. Then with a crunch of metal, it smashed into rock and stopped. So did Dad, as he scratched his head and surveyed the damage. This then was how they became friends.

Matt had two children, Mike and Christina, who loved us and had been trying to get their father to get them a pup. On this particular day, passing by, we saw that they'd got their way. And a little tearaway he was too, running in circles and jumping up at Dix and me.

"He's sweet," remarked Dad. "Got a name for him?"

"Doggy," replied Matt.

That's original, I thought, and Dad just said, "Oh."

After that day, he'd come with us on our romp and Dad would drop him off to Matt on our way home. We don't see much of him these days as Matt couldn't keep an eye on him and work at the same time, so he left him at his house with the family where, I'm pleased to say, he's been given a proper name… Billy! A bit silly and confusing, I thought, as half the goats in the neighbourhood were called Billy! Matt's children bring him round sometimes to play. We look forward to these days, as they never forget to bring us a snack.

So, where was I? Oh yes – our walks. Just before the track leading to Matt's, there's a rubbish skip and, as we were passing one day, I caught a movement out of the corner of my eye. Turning round, I saw this tiny furry thing coming from under the skip... and then another... and another.

"Wow! Look at this!" I cried. "Three kittens!"

Well, I'd heard about kittens – young cats they are – and cats are not supposed to like dogs, are they? But these three didn't seem to know about that as they rubbed themselves against us and made soft sounds of contentment. Pretty things they were, but each was of a different colouring – one ginger, a grey one with a white stripe around its neck, and one black and white.

"Where have you lot come from?" I asked.

"Well" cried Grey. "We're not exactly sure. We'd been with our mum for some time. Under some tree, we were. Then, one night, someone appeared, put the three of us in a box and dumped us here. Why would they do that? And where's our mum?" And with that, he burst into tears.

"There, there," said Dixie. "We'll take care of you and I'm sure our Dad'll try to find out where you've come from and what's happened to your mum."

Dad looked at me and said, "Harry, you hold the fort whilst I go and get them something to eat and drink. I'll be as quick as I can."

Well our house was pretty near, and he was back before you could say Jack Russell. Putting two bowls down, the kittens tucked in and as we started our walk, I turned to them and said, "Listen you lot! Stay here under the trees and don't go near the road. It's dangerous! We'll be back later."

When we got back home, Dad told our Mum all about it. Then, just before nightfall, Dad and I went up the road to refill the kittens' bowls. I repeated my warning about the road and added, "Now, eat up, snuggle up, and we'll see you tomorrow."

The following morning, I couldn't wait to see the kittens again and I think Dad felt the same as we set out early for our walk, together with fresh victuals. They came scurrying out from under the tree when they heard us coming.

"Any news of our mum?" asked Ginger.

"Not yet," I replied, "but be sure our Dad's working on it."

"It's early days yet," piped Poppy.

"Yes," joined in Dixie. "I'm sure we'll find her."

"So, keep safe and don't worry," I said. "Everything will be fine. See you later, guys."

Later that evening, I heard our Mum and Dad discussing them.

"I mean we can't just leave them there," our Mum said. "That's a dangerous corner."

"I agree," said Dad. "But if you're thinking what I think you're thinking, forget it! We've a full house. I'll ask around and see if I can find a home for them."

Dad was right, of course. Where would they all sleep? There was enough fighting going on at night as to who got the most comfortable basket. Poppy always seemed to get the best because she retired first and boy, once she was down, nobody could budge her. I was always last in after doing the rounds and checking to see that all was well. So I got the basket with the lumpy cushion. Imagine the chaos with another three! Yes Dad – good idea!

In a way, the problem was solved for us, although not in the way we would have liked. The next morning only Grey came out to meet us. Look as we might, the other two had disappeared – not a sign of them anywhere.

"What happened?" I asked Grey. "Where have they gone?"

Grey was sobbing his heart out. "I don't know," he cried. "We all curled up together last night, but when I awoke they were gone. I've looked everywhere."

Dad and Pops spent ages searching, but they had obviously gone.

"This is silly," said Pops. "Why would anyone want to take two and leave one behind?"

"It is very strange," added Dixie. "What'll we do with Grey?"

"Well," I replied, "we'll have to leave that up to dad and I've an idea what he'll do."

"Do you think that...?" stuttered Dixie.

"You don't mean..." joined in Pops.

"Yes I do," I said. "I think we'll get a new member of the family."

And so it was. Dad bent down and, picking him up, said, "Come on. We can't leave you here on your own, can we?"

So we started off homewards.

"Oh dear," said Pops. "Bang goes our walk again!"

"Don't be like that," scolded Dixie. "We must take him home. He's far too young to be left on his own."

"Yeah," I said. "But don't worry – I'll bet you a bone to a biscuit that Dad dumps him with Mum and we get our walk. He loves it as much as we do!"

So our family grew by one. He was given the name of Alfie, and we all agreed that it suited him. He was a mischievous little fella and, somehow, it was a mischievous sounding name. Boy, did he give us dogs the run around, never seeming to tire. He had to be taught a few manners though, and got more than one biff from me. Several times I saw him with a tear in his eye, and it was obvious he was missing his family.

"I do miss them so," he sobbed. "What could have happened to them?"

Trying to comfort him, I said, "Look Alfie, think about it this way – where we discovered you was a dangerous corner, with cars screaming by all the time. I doubt if any of you would have survived for very long. So, if somebody took them, and that's what I think happened, then they'll be much better off. Why, they're probably lapping a bowl of milk this very moment and wondering where you are."

This seemed to cheer him up a little.

"Yes," he sighed. "I'm sure you're right, Harry. Thank you. I feel a bit better now."

Even so, every time we passed that spot we couldn't help but look around.

We were all good friends by now and spent many an hour playing tag or hide –and seek. At the end of one such day, Alfie wanted to know all about us and was amazed to learn that we had all been rescued.

"Yup. This is the original orphans' home," quipped Pops.

"Well then, aren't I the lucky one?" answered Alfie.

We told him how Dixie had lost her sight and Poppy her ears.

"I don't see much wrong with you though, Harry," Alfie pointed out.

"He doesn't talk about it," said Pops, and both girls broke into fits of laughter.

"The unkindest cut of all," added Dixie and they screamed even louder.

"All right, that's enough girls," I said, feeling my face turn red.

Just then, Mum called us in for our evening meal, but it was some time before they could control themselves.

Chapter 9

Where Eagles Dare

One morning, coming back from our daily walk, our Mum met Dad exclaiming, "Alfie's nowhere to be found!"

"Don't worry too much. I expect he is exploring somewhere in the garden," said Dad. Even so, I saw a worried look on his face.

Actually, I thought that Alfie was probably sulking somewhere because earlier Dad wouldn't take him on a walk with us. You should have seen the carry on.

"Why can't I come?" he wailed to me. "I can keep up with you lot and I wouldn't get lost, so what's the problem?"

"I'll tell you what the problem is," I replied. "The first stretch is on a busy road and for that we're all put on a harness and leash. And besides, with your short legs, you'd never make it."

"Yes I would," he screamed. "And anyway, why can't I have a harness?"

"Because," I explained, "they don't make them that small."

"Course they do!" he shouted. "What about small dogs, eh? Small dogs have them."

"Not that small," I replied.

"Course they do! What about puppies, eh? Puppies have them!"

And so he carried on until I lost my cool.

"Look, shut up! When you are bigger and stronger I know Dad will take you with us. For now, stay here – we've got to go." And off we went, leaving him fuming as Mum shut him in the lounge.

Anyway, as I was saying, Alfie had never gone missing before and so we were all a bit concerned.

"Oh dear! I hope he's alright," Dixie said. "Remember what the crows told us about the eagles and how dangerous they were, and Alfie's such a little fella!"

"Gosh!" said Pops. "Perish the thought! C'mon, let's ask around – see if anybody knows anything."

Well we looked around and asked around.

"Haven't seen him," said the crows.

"Nope, haven't seen him," added the sparrows.

Then a voice said, "Look, I don't want to worry you, but I've seen some eagles hovering overhead."

Turning round, we saw a small hedgehog.

"You must be Spikey," I said.

"S'right," he answered, "and you'll be Harry. Heard about you I have – but about them eagles…"

"Oh dear!" cried Dixie. "I fear the worst."

"Now, now Dix," I said. "Let's not jump to conclusions. I'm sure he would have spotted them and hidden somewhere."

"D'you really think he's that clever?" snorted Pops. "He'd probably wave and want to play."

I glared at her. "It's not time to be funny, Pops. This is serious! C'mon, let's look some more. See you later, Spikey – we'll come and visit you."

We were just about to move on when a voice stopped us.

"S'cuse me, but I think I saw him." Turning round, there stood a badger.

"You saw him? Where did you see him?" I asked.

The badger shuffled closer. "Is he a little grey fella with white round his neck?" he asked.

"That's him," replied Pops. "Where did you see him?"

"Well," replied the badger, "I was just coming out of my hole when this dog came charging along, nearly knocking me over. Seen him before I have – white. Young hooligan."

"That would be Billy," I said.

"Yeah, well," continued the badger, "I had just got my balance when this little fella went flying after him. Went up that way, they did," he said pointing.

"Thanks Badger," I said.

"Think nothing of it," he replied. "Bobby's the name, and helping's me game."

Setting off in the direction that Bobby had pointed, I realised that we were headed towards Matteaus' workshop from another angle. Matteaus was Billy's boss, of course, so it all made sense – Billy had gone to find Matteaus and Alfie had followed.

I was right! Coming out of the olive grove near the workshop, there they both were, chasing each other around. I didn't see Matteaus, although his truck was there so he was probably round the back, tending his chickens or rabbits or whatever else he kept there. The proverbial farmyard, this was!

"Oi," I called to Alfie. "What do you mean by running off like that? Your Mum's frantic with worry!"

"Now hold on a bit, Harry," said Billy as we approached. "It's not like that."

"No it's not," blurted out Alfie. "I'm lucky to be alive. Can I tell it, Billy?" he asked.

"Yes, go on," Billy replied.

"You see," began Alfie, "some time after you left, our Mum let me out, but I got pretty bored with no one to play with. Well, I kind of wandered around and found myself in the clearing near the top of the hill."

"Yes, I know it," said Pops.

"So, I was about halfway across when it suddenly got darker, like the sun going behind a cloud, you know? Well, I knew there were clear blue skies, so I looked up and… Oh Lordy! There were these three monsters looking down at me! Eagles!"

"Had one lost an eye?" I interrupted.

"Yeah, that's right," answered Alfie.

"Oh blimey!" I cried. "That'd be Ike and his two sons, Elmer and Floyd, the Feather Gang! Carry on, Alf."

"Well, I knew I was in trouble, so I veered to the left, running as fast as I could. But they kept pace with me, descending all the time. I raced away to the right but it was no good – they just followed, getting closer all the time. Suddenly, I had nowhere to go as I crashed into a tree. They quickly landed and had me surrounded."

"Oh heavens!" cried Dixie. "How awful! You must have been so frightened."

"I was that," replied Alfie. "My heart was pounding and my legs were playing Alexander's Ragtime Band! Then one of them spoke.

"'Ho ho! What have we here? Could it be lunch?'

"'Lunch?' I said. 'You'll be lunch if Harry sees you.'

"'But Harry's not going to see us, is he?' they chorused.

"I was feeling more than a bit nervous, I can tell you, but determined not to show it. I said, 'I'll tell him what you're up to!' They just glared at me and the old one said,

"'I don't think that you'll be telling anyone again.'

"Suddenly, a voice cried out and Billy came charging along, knocking them every which way.

"'C'mon Alfie,' he yelled. 'This way', and we ran like the wind, reaching the thick foliage before they could recover. Their bulk didn't allow them to follow, but we heard them, snarling and arguing with one another before they took to the sky. Billy brought me here and was about to take me home when you all arrived. So now you know."

"Yes," I said, "and now you know how dangerous it can be to go out on your own."

"Whew!" said Dixie. "That's quite a story!"

"Yes," added Pops. "Good old Billy."

"You're quite a hero, my boy," I said. "Come on, Alfie, let's get you home – our Mum and Dad will be wondering where we all are. In the meantime, I've got to think of a plan to sort out old Ike and his boys."

Funny thing was, we never saw the Feather Gang again. Some said they left town when they heard I was looking for them. Some said that old Ike was shot by a hunter and his two boys moved on. Whatever – we were pleased to see the back of them!

Chapter 10
Red

As summer turned to autumn and the days grew cooler, we had the first rain. Now, if there was one thing Alfie hated it was water, so when it rained no way could you get him out of the house. During the summer, Dad bought him a harness and lead and, true to his word, he kept up with us, loving every minute. But, when it rained, forget it!

"I'll see you when you get back," he would say. "Think of me in my nice, dry, warm basket."

Actually, it wasn't a good time for him to be out. In fact, it wasn't a good time for any of us to be out. It was olive picking time! Olives flying all over the place, bonking you on the head! Tractors and trucks everywhere, falling branches, not to mention the fires, which happened when the old branches were cut off and bonfires made of them.

Anyway, one day when it rained and there was no olive picking because of it, Dad took us the short walk up by Matt's workshop, leaving Alfie in his warm, dry basket. Just before we got to the workshop, it really poured and we scampered to get shelter. Matt was inside, and so was a small ginger cat.

"Come in out of the rain," shouted Matt.

"Hello, Matt," said Dad. "Thanks. We're soaked."

As we approached, Pops said, "I'm sure that's one of the kittens that went missing. Bigger, but I'm sure it's him."

"Me too," I agreed.

At that moment, the cat shouted, "Hey, fellas! Is it really you? Remember me?"

"My goodness!" said Pops. "Of course we remember you. Where have you come from? More to the point, where have you been?"

"It's a long story," answered Ginger.

"Where's the cat come from?" I heard Dad ask Matt. "I think I've seen him before."

"You have?" enquired Matt.

"Well, I've seen it wandering around the village looking lost for a couple of days now. I asked around, but nobody seemed to know where it's come from. When I saw it this morning, soaking wet, I picked it up and brought it here."

"You only saw one?" asked Dad.

"Yes," replied Matt. "Why do you ask?"

"Well," said Dad, "if he's who I think he is, then there's another one." And he explained the story of the kittens.

"I'll keep a look out for it," said Matt.

"Thanks, Matt, you do that. Anyway, we've got to get going. See you around," said Dad as he trudged off.

I hung back a bit and whispered to Ginger, "We'll see you later, and we might just have a surprise for you. Hang in there." And I ran to catch up with the others.

By the time we got home we were drenched, and Mum was waiting for us with a load of towels.

"Dry them off before they come in, and take those shoes off," she demanded. "I don't want muddy paws or shoes on my nice clean floors."

It was good to have a brisk rub down and get warm.

"Have a nice walk, did you?" smiled Alfie, suddenly appearing. "Got all cold and wet, did you?"

"Oh, be quiet, Alfie!" scolded Dixie. "What's wrong with you anyway, not coming out in the rain? Scared of shrinking, are you?"

"Maybe he is 'cos if he got any smaller he'd disappear" quipped Poppy, and we all laughed.

"Yeah, yeah. Well, you can all laugh but you have to admit that it's better to be warm and dry than cold and wet," purred Alfie.

"Oh, I don't know," I said. "You might be warm and dry inside, but inside you don't get to see the things that are outside," and I gave Pops a wink.

"What things?" asked Alfie. "And what was that wink for? What did you see?"

"Oh, just things," Poppy said, airily.

"No, no," said Alfie. "Not just things. You've seen something, haven't you?"

"Food time," shouted Dad.

"Oh good," said Pops. "I'm starving."

"You're always starving," laughed Dixie. "C'mon, Alfie, let's eat!"

"Yes," I added, "and, if you're a good little boy, we'll tell you all about the things on our walk."

Well, Alfie gobbled his food and walked up and down, waiting for us to finish.

"Come on! Come on!" he yelled. "Tell me! Tell me!"

"We said if you were a good little boy," announced Dixie.

"Oh, I am! I'm good! I'm really good!" grinned Alfie. "So what happened? What did you see?" He was beside himself.

"Well, we'd show you," said Pops, "but it's too late now. It's dark. You'd never see him."

"See him? See who?"

"Ginger."

"Ginger? Who's Ginger?"

"Ginger. Your long lost brother," I said.

"Gin... You mean Red? You've seen Red? I don't believe it!" stammered Alfie.

"Yup! Up by Matt's," said Dixie.

"Red?" I asked. "Is that what you called him?"

"Yes," replied Alfie. "You see, we all gave each other a name. He was named Red because of his colour. Our sister we called Dotty because she's as mad as a hatter, and I was known as The Preacher because of the white stripe around my neck – but never mind that. How was he? And was Dotty with him? When can I see him?"

"Now hold on, Alfie. You'll have to wait until morning. We can sneak away early when Dad lets us out, I promise. And no, sorry – Dotty wasn't with him. You'll have to be patient. Now let's get some sleep."

"Patient? Sleep?" shouted Alfie. "How do you expect me to sleep? Oh, if only it were morning," he groaned.

"It'll come soon enough," said Dixie. "Now try to relax."

We settled down for the night, but I was awakened several times by Alfie murmuring in his sleep.

At first light I gave Dad a couple of nudges.

"For goodness' sake, Harry! It's too early! Go back to sleep," he mumbled.

As he turned over, I thought, no way! We have to get going. I nudged him again and gave him one of my best whines.

"Oh, Harry!" he yawned. "Come on then. No peace for the wicked." And putting on his slippers, he opened up.

Alfie zipped out between us and I had to call him to wait for the girls.

"Hold it, Alf. You know how long it takes them to get ready. Now, just wait."

Eventually they emerged, bleary eyed.

When we were all assembled, I said, "Right. Now, keep together and mind the road." And off we went.

All was okay until we got off the road, and then Alfie could contain himself no longer. He dashed up the track towards Matt's, leaving us in his wake. Phew! He could run! Poor old Dixie couldn't go that fast and, naturally, we kept to her pace. When we arrived at the workshop, we were confronted by an unexpected scene. Red was inside looking out, and Alfie was outside looking in! Matt hadn't opened up yet. We hadn't thought of that. Anyway, they were having a right old chinwag through the glass. How are you? – Where have you been? – and blah, blah, blah.

"When will Matt open up?" Alfie wanted to know.

"Well, I've only been here a couple of days," explained Red, "but he seems to get here early. He's got a lot of work on."

"Maybe we'd better leave and come back later. Our Mum and Dad will wonder where we are."

"No! No! NO!" shouted Alfie. "You go, but I can't leave now!"

At that very moment, Matt's truck came into the yard.

"He's here! He's here!" shouted Alfie.

As Matt climbed out of the truck he said, "Hello! What are you lot doing here without your Dad? He'll be worr... Ah! I think I see! You've come to see the kitty, haven't you?"

And as he opened the workshop door, Red came flying out, straight into Alfie's arms. Well, they hugged and they danced around, laughing and crying at the same time.

"Oh dear," sniffed Dixie. "I think I'm going to cry too."

"Me too!" choked Pops.

It was very touching, and I must admit to having to fight back the tears.

Not wishing the girls to know that, I said, "I'm sorry, but it's time we were leaving. C'mon Alfie."

"Okay, coming, coming. Just one thing, Red – what about Dotty, or shouldn't I ask?"

"She was alright the last time I saw her, but we've got to get her out!"

"Out?" said Alfie. "Out of where?"

"C'mon Alfie," I called. "Let's go."

"Right. Coming. Red, we'll be right back and you can tell me all. See you soon."

With that, we all set off for home.

"Gosh, I'm hungry," said Dixie.

"Tell me about it!" complained Pops.

Eating breakfast, Mum told us that Dad had to go into town and, as she was busy with housework, we would have to amuse ourselves. This suited us just fine, as we would be able to see Red. Our luck was in! Finishing breakfast, we hurried off.

"Now, what's this about?" I asked. "Fill us in with all the details, from the moment you were taken from The Preacher... Er, I mean Alfie."

Red began, "No, see, we weren't actually taken away. No, not then. See, The Preacher – that is, Alfie – was snoring so loudly we couldn't sleep so we went for a walk. It was just getting light and we went up the track leading here."

"You're mad!" interrupted Pops. "So many hazards! You could have been killed!"

"Yes," I added, "and I told you to stay where you were when we first saw you."

"Yeah, well, let's just say we forgot. Anyway, we walked right past here and down the other side. Then we got a bit lost with all the different tracks. Spotting a couple of crows, we asked the way.

"'Just follow that track,' they said, and they pointed. 'But for goodness' sake, watch out for the eagles. If they see you, you're history.'

"Thanking them, we kept well in to the side of the road where we thought we'd be hidden from above. Well, the eagles didn't see us, but the man in the truck did. He stopped, got out and before you could say Jack Russell he picked us up and put us in a dirty old sack. Gee, it was scary! Dark and stuffy. After a while, we stopped and the man picked up the sack. The next thing we knew, we were poured out of the sack onto the ground, which was surrounded by a high wire fence. To make matters worse, there was a little black dog that I didn't like the look of, although he was on a chain. He turned out to be a good friend, though."

"Um," I mused. "A little black dog, you say? He didn't have a brightly coloured collar, did he?

"Why yes," replied Red. "How on earth did you know that?"

"That sounds like Old Angus who went missing some weeks ago. He belongs to Sylvia and Dimitri who live up the way. They were heartbroken when he went missing. We'd never met him, but I heard Mum and Dad talking about it."

"Yes, Angus," said Red excitedly. "Angus was his name. Got a strange way of talking. Told us of how this man lured him with some kind words, then grabbed him and dumped him, like us."

"What's he doing, nicking all us animals?" cried Pops.

"No idea," replied Red, "but he was horrible. Never let us out and hardly fed us."

"Yes, I can see that," added Pops. "You're very skinny."

"Skinny!" shouted Red. "You should see poor old Angus – his collar's nearly falling over his head!"

"Poor things!" said Dixie. "We'll have to do something!"

"Yes, well, that's what I was getting to," answered Red. "One day Angus says to me, 'Red, we've gotta get out of here. I cannae do much chained up like this, but you can, Red!'"

"What did you do?" asked Pops.

"Hold on and I'll tell you," replied Red. "Angus showed me how I was to dig with my front paws to make a hole."

"Gosh, that was clever," said Dixie.

"Yes," agreed Red. "So one day, when the coast was clear, I started to make a hole by the fence with Dotty helping me."

"How long did it take the two of you?" I asked.

"Well, not so long," replied Red. "It had been raining so the earth was soft."

"That was lucky," said Pops.

"Yes, it was," replied Red. "When it was big enough to squeeze through, I told Dotty to stay and look after poor Angus, and promised the pair of them that I'd return as fast as I could with help. Then off I ran."

"Wow," said Dixie. "How did you know which way to go?"

"Well, I didn't," replied Red. "I wandered around all over the place until I came to the village. Again, I wandered around trying to get my bearings. Then, on the second day – pouring with rain it was – this man picked me up and I thought, 'Oh, no! Not again!'. But I needn't have worried – he was kind. Brought me here, he did, dried me and gave me food and a drink. So here I am. That's it."

"Wow," said Dixie. "That's quite a story."

"Yes, it is," agreed Pops. "So, what are we going to do about Angus and Dotty?"

"Um," I said. "Red, any chance you find that place again?"

"Well, yes, I think so," replied Red. "I noted several landmarks, so I'll give it a try."

"Right," I said. "We'll just have to go AWOL. We've got to rescue them. We'll have to choose our days well. Like today, when Mum's busy and Dad's in town."

"But it might take more than a day!" wailed Alfie, "and we can't go missing overnight! Our Mum and Dad would have a fit!"

"You're right," I agreed. "So we'll have to do it in stages. Find a landmark, pick up a scent, then come back, and so on and so on until we've got the whole route. Once we've got that, we go straight there, get them out and head for home."

"That's a great idea," said Dixie. "And, talking about home, we must be getting back."

"You're right," I said. "Let's go! Red, we'll see you tomorrow – hopefully with a plan of action."

Chapter 11

The Great Escape

The following day we weren't able to see Red as it was a sunny day and Dad took us to Limenaria by the sea. It's a great walk and always ends with a swim, so I wasn't complaining.

But I was anxious to contact Red so, when we got back, I sent Alfie to see him to tell him not to worry, and that we would see him for sure as Dad was going to town and would be away for the day. In the meantime, he was to get to the village and see if he could pick up any scent. I figured this might save us some time – and so it was.

On seeing him the next morning, he was beside himself with excitement.

"I got a good scent," he explained. "And I'm sure I know the right direction to take."

"Right," I said, and turned to Pops. "Pops, you go with Red and see what you can find. Dixie and I will have to get back, but Mum knows you often go walkabout, so you won't be missed. Off you go now, you two, and good luck." And with that they scampered off.

A couple of hours later, Pops arrived at the house and I could tell by the look on her face that it was good news.

"Okay," she said. "We found them! Couldn't believe how easy it was. Neither could Red. He recognised all the landmarks and, before we knew it, there they were! So Red went and had a word whilst I kept a lookout. It seems tomorrow would be perfect for the breakout as it's Sunday and this guy always goes out for the day. Whew! I'm hungry! How long 'til food?"

Typical Pops, I thought, always thinking of her stomach, no matter what else is going on in the world.

"Right gang," I said. "Listen up. Tomorrow it is, then. Dad works in town tonight and stays over. When he gets back, he's too tired to take us out 'til after lunch, so that should give us enough time."

"Ooh," gasped Dixie. "Isn't it exciting!"

"It is that, Dix," I answered. "Now, Alfie, you run up and tell Red to meet us down here as early as he can. Going straight from here will save time."

"How are we going to release Angus if he's on a chain?" asked Pops.

"We'll worry about that when the time comes," I answered. "So let's take it easy for now. Tomorrow could be a long day."

Alfie returned to say that Red would be waiting outside for us. At six o'clock Dad said goodbye, saying he would see us about ten the following day. He'd stay overnight at our old house, and memories came flooding back of Mia, Scruffy, Max, Henry and Stelios. Oh, how I missed them all.

Early Sunday morning, I had to nudge our Mum several times before she stirred.

"Oh, Harry," she groaned. "It's Sunday! Can't I lie in for a bit?" and turned over.

So I gave her another nudge and one of my best whines – that did the trick. Murmuring something I didn't understand, she hopped out of bed and let us all out. Red was standing patiently by the gate and, after waiting some minutes for the girls to get themselves ready, off we went.

In the village, we got some strange looks from early risers. I suppose we did look a motley crew. Anyway, I shouldn't think it's every day that you see three dogs and two cats charging down the road together. Once through the village, Red and Pops led the way, and after about twenty minutes of twists and turns, we arrived. There they were, and Dotty and Angus let out a cheer when they saw us.

"Boy, are we glad to see you," said Dotty. "The man has gone for the day so we should have plenty of time."

"That's good to know," I said. "Right! Here's the plan. Dixie, You've the best ears so you stay here and be the listen out. Alfie and Red, you stay with her and be the lookouts. Between you we'll have plenty of warning if someone should come. Pops, you come with me." And together we approached the fence.

"There," I pointed. "Okay Pops, let's get digging – and remember, it's got to be big enough to get me in. Let's go!"

We dug furiously, deeper and deeper, wider and wider.

"Phew!" I said. "I'm getting too old for this!"

"Nah," replied Pops. "You're just not fit enough – carrying too much weight. Better go on a diet!" She laughed and Angus and Dotty joined in.

Looking over at Dixie, Red and Alfie, I shouted, "Everything okay?"

"All clear," they yelled in unison.

"Good," said Pops. "We won't be long, if Aitch can last the pace."

"Okay, big head," I said. "Race you to the other side!"

We both put our backs into it and then we were through. Dotty couldn't contain herself and went charging through the tunnel to be reunited with Alfie and Red. It was wonderful to see them all hugging and kissing. Meantime, we had a problem – how to release old Angus as he was chained to a pole.

"Any ideas, Pops?" I asked.

"I've one, laddie" said Angus.

"What's that?" I asked.

"Well, no," he replied. "Since I've been strugglin' to get oot, I've noticed that there's movement in yon pole. I reckon with me pullin' and you pushin' we can get it over on its side and slide the chain off the end. What d'you think?"

"Brilliant!" I said. "Let's go!" and we put every ounce into it.

Slowly but surely, the pole loosened until it toppled onto its side. The chain slid off and Angus ran free.

"Och, laddie, yer did it!" he shouted. "Now let's get away' oot o' here before yon mon gets back."

Once through the hole, I turned to Angus and said, "Okay, you go and join the rest. Pops and I still have some work to do. C'mon Pops, you know where to go."

"That I do," answered Pops.

Together we ran into the garden and started pulling up everything we found – plants, flowers, vegetables – you name it. By the time we'd finished, it looked like a herd of elephants had run amok. Finally, I turned on the hose with my teeth and left the water running everywhere.

"Good work, Aitch," said Pops.

"Not half bad, Pops," I replied. "That'll teach him to mess with us 'dumb' animals!" And we both had a good laugh before we ran and joined the others.

As we passed the church in the village, crowds of people were emerging after the Sunday service. There were astonished looks among them and a feeling of excitement at the unique scene of four dogs and three cats hurtling by.

Finally, we stopped to get our breath some hundred metres from our house.

"Well," spoke Angus, "I did not meet ya afore, Harry, but everyone spoke highly of ya and now I can see why."

"Glad to help you oot – er, out. But you must thank the whole gang – they all played their part. Tell me something that I've been itching to ask you. You have a very strange accent and speak words that I don't understand. What's that all about?"

"Well," answered Angus. "My Dad, Dimitri, is from hereabouts, but my Mum comes from Scotland, and although she's been here many years, you wouldn't ken – know – it so I guess some of it rubbed off onto me," he laughed.

"Well, I find it very attractive," said Dixie.

"Hey, Dix," grinned Pops. "Are you sure it's not Angus that you find attractive?" And we all roared with laughter.

"So," I announced. "It's time for us to go our separate ways. Dotty, you go with Red. You'll both be well looked after by Matt and his children, and we'll see you nearly every day on our walks. Angus, good luck my friend. We'll be seeing you too."

"Aye, that ya will," said Angus. "I'll be on ma way, the noo. I cannae wait at see my Mum and Dad's faces. Bye."

"Hold on a minute, Angus," I said. "Listen, all of you. Look out for yourselves. I don't want to go through all that again!"

Once again, we all laughed and went on our way.

We were near Sylvia and Dimitri's some days later on our morning walk, when Angus came running over – a very smart Angus. He had on a new collar and was about twelve shades lighter than before.

"Hello Angus," I shouted. "Wow! Do you look smart?"

"Aye, well I've had three baths, had a haircut and blow dry."

"Not to mention the new collar," added Alfie.

"You look great," joined in Poppy.

"Aye, well I feel guid – that's a fact – and it's grand to be home. But I've no time to myself! They watch me all the time and…"

"Angus, Angus," a voice shouted. "Where are you? Come on!"

"See what I mean?" said Angus. "That's her the noo, so I'd best be off. Guid to see ya. Come around some time. My folks would love te see all of yous. 'Bye the noo." And he was gone.

Chapter 12

The Colour Of Money

It was getting near the end of the year and there was great excitement in the air – Christmas was coming!

Our Mum and Dad had decorated the lounge with lanterns and paper chains. Christmas cards were everywhere sent by friends from near and far. Then, on shopping day, Dad brought home a Christmas tree which Mum dressed with silver and gold balls, coloured lights that blinked on and off and, finally, an angel perched right on the top. It was really lovely.

"I wonder how long it will be before Alfie knocks the coloured balls off?" quipped Poppy.

"I wouldn't like to be in his shoes if he does!" replied Dixie.

Joining the debate, I said, "I don't think he'll see Christmas if he touches that tree!"

Coming through the door, Alfie said, "I heard that! No, I promise to be good – but it'll be hard." And we all had to laugh.

Christmas Day promised to be memorable. Fred and Doris, together with Doris' parents, had been invited for the feast. The dinner would consist of roast turkey with a pile of veg, Christmas pudding and special drinks. Our Mum would lay the table, putting on a brightly coloured cloth, candles would be lit and there would be crackers! Not our favourite toy! They make a loud bang, making us all jump out of our skins. Spare a thought for poor Poppy, who hated loud noises, and Alfie, who wouldn't know what was going on. But they are essential, as they contained not only a small gift but also a funny paper hat, and it wouldn't be Christmas without a funny hat, would it?

Before dinner, everyone would exchange presents with oohs and ahs, 'thank you's, 'just what I needed', hugs and kisses. After dinner, our Dad would play the piano and everybody would sing! Yes, it was going to be a right old knees-up!

Now, I remembered that, after breakfast, our Mum and Dad would give presents to each other and to us before clearing away the wrapping paper to start preparing for the day. The dinner was scheduled for three o'clock, but there was a lot to be done beforehand.

We'd seen our Mum and Dad wrapping up presents for some days now and, with only a couple of days 'til Christmas Day, I called the gang together.

"Listen up," I said. "Everybody will be giving out presents except us. We've got nothing to give our Mum and Dad. That's not right. They deserve something, don't you agree?"

"Yes," answered Pops. "But to buy presents you need money. How are we going to get money?"

"That's been troubling me," I said. "And I can come up with only one answer. We'll have to somehow take it from our Mum's purse."

"What?" burst out Dixie. "You can't do that! That's stealing!"

"It wouldn't *exactly* be stealing, would it?" answered Alfie. "I mean, it's not for *us*, is it? It's to buy them presents."

"Well… Putting it that way, I suppose it would be alright," said Dixie cautiously.

"And we won't take *too* much" added Pops. "How much do you think?"

"Ten euros?" I asked.

"Yes, that should do it," answered Dixie.

"Alright, agreed," I said. "Ten euros to buy the presents."

"That's all very well," put in Dixie, "but where are we going to buy the gifts? I mean, there are no shops around here, apart from Katerina's Mini Market."

"I know that," I said. "We'll have to go to Agios Nikolaos."

"Ag Nik?" yelled Pops. "But that's miles away!"

"By road, yes," I stated. "But if we go as the crow flies, it's not so far."

"But I can't fly," cried Alfie.

"Silly!" said Dixie. "As the crow flies means to take the direct route overland. Can't fly! Really! Where do you come from? Anyway, I don't think your little legs would make it."

"Well, you don't think I'm going to stay here and miss out on all the fun, do you? No! I'm coming. Don't you worry about my legs – they'll make it."

"Look, it'll be a long trip," I said. "So we'll all have to help one another along. There's only two days to go, so it must be tomorrow, bright and early. But first – the money!"

Our Mum kept her wallet in a large bag which generally lived on the lounge table. Dad said that he was amazed how she found anything in it 'cos he said it housed everything but the kitchen sink. A joke it was, but it could have presented a problem to us until Alfie came up with an idea.

"I'm small and my eyes are made for the dark," he told us. "So, since it's black in there and the best time for the snatch is during the night, I'll get in, find it and fish it out. How's that sound?"

"Sound as a pound," I answered.

So, that night when the house was asleep, us four crept into the lounge. Earlier Pops had told us that the bag was on the table, as usual, so Alfie immediately jumped up and disappeared inside. Seconds later, as our eyes became accustomed to the dark, we saw Alfie's rear end emerging as he gradually pulled on the wallet. Then, with a final jerk, it came flying out, left the table and, with dull thud, hit the floor. We held our breath for a moment but all was quiet – Mum and Dad hadn't stirred.

The next part would be a bit more tricky – getting the money out of the wallet!

This was where Poppy came in. Going to the wallet, she bared her teeth, grabbed a corner and gently unfolded it. There it was, the money! Only thing was, being stuffed in the wallet, you couldn't tell one note from another. How would we choose a ten euro note correctly?

"Pops," I said. "You'll just have to pull one out and hope for the best!"

"Right. Here goes." And she slowly pulled a note out. Well, in the dark, we still didn't know if it was a ten euro note or not.

"We'll just have to wait 'til first light," I said. "Meantime, let's get the wallet back in the bag."

This was done swiftly with the precision of a good team – Poppy closed it, I picked it up and put it on the table, then Alfie pulled it back into the bag.

"No sweat," said Pops.

"Great work," added Dixie. "It went smoothly. I've no doubt you chose the right note." And so it was.

As dawn broke, we let out a sigh of relief to see a ten euro note. Poppy scrunched it up and secured it under my collar. We were ready!

Chapter 13

A Christmas Story

It was seven o'clock on Christmas Eve morning that we set off for Ag Nik. Well, that is, after we waited an age for the girls to get ready.

"Come on you two!" I growled.

"Okay. We're coming! It's not every day that us girls get to go to town, and we want to look pretty," explained Dixie as they arrived.

"Can't see much difference," laughed Alfie.

"You shush," said Pops, and I had to grin as we started out.

"Stick close to me, Dixie" I said. "There'll be a lot of rough terrain. Listen for my bell."

"You sure you know where you're going?" cracked Alfie.

"Course he does," scolded Pops. "Trust old Aitch."

"We head due west, and not so much of the 'old' thank you," I chided.

I knew it was due west and I knew you had to keep the sea on the right, but I also knew that it was possible to lose direction in the hills. As we pressed on, I said a quiet little prayer to St. Francis and St. Christopher.

At that precise moment, Poppy stopped, nudged me and said, "Look, Aitch! Ahead! There's a bird flying right for us. Look out! He's going to hit us!"

And we all ducked as he flew inches over us at great speed.

"Crazy bird!" I cried. "What's he doing?"

We watched as he climbed to a great height, turned, and then dived straight towards us.

"He's coming again!" yelled Alfie. "RUN!"

But as we were about to, the bird pulled out of the dive, did a loop-thee-loop and skidded to a halt in front of us.

"Hiya fellas," he said.

"Jonathan Livingstone Seagull!" I said, open-mouthed. "What are you doing here?"

Seeing that bird filled my heart with joy. We often talked about him and his exploits in the sky.

"Well," he said, "I was on my way to see you and wish you all a Happy Christmas."

"Thank you, Jon," said Dixie. "And the same to you."

"Thanks, Dix, and I bring greetings from the gang," he continued. "Scruffy, Mia, Henry, Stelios and Max."

"Gee, that's nice," I said. "How are they all?"

"They're fine, apart from Max who's got a problem with his back legs, but then he is getting on a bit. Nevertheless, he often comes to join us for a swim. But tell me about yourselves. I see the family's grown."

"Yes," I said. "That's Poppy and over there's Alfie. Poppy, Alfie, meet Jonathan Livingstone Seagull, a friend from the past and king of the skies."

"Good to meet you," said Alfie.

"Yes," added Pops. "Aitch and Dixie speak of you often."

"Aitch?" inquired Jon.

"Harry, I mean," explained Poppy. "Aitch is his nickname, which is a long story."

"Tell me about it sometime," said Jon. "Now, where are you off to?"

"Well," I said. "We're off to Ag Nik to buy presents for our Mum and Dad."

"Wow," said Jon. "That's quite a trip, and you're a little bit off course."

"Are we?" I asked, somewhat surprised.

"Yes – not much though. You should head due west, and at the moment, you're heading southwest. Don't worry, I'll guide you there, but we'd better get a move on. It's a long round trip and you don't want to be out here in the dark! So, watch me." So saying, he took to the sky, with us following in his direction.

On and on we went, keeping Jon in sight at all times, until we reached the outskirts of Ag Nik. Just then, Jonathan landed next to us.

"Right. What are we looking for?"

"A shop," replied Poppy.

"A shop, she says!" cried Alfie. "Of course, a shop! What kind of shop, Aitch?"

"Well, Mum spends a lot of time reading, so I guess a bookshop," I replied.

"Right, a bookshop it is," said Jonathan. "You wait here and I'll see what I can find." With that, he soared into the sky once more.

"Aren't we lucky to have him with us?" remarked Dixie.

"Yes, indeed," I replied. "Without him it would have… Hello, here he comes, back already. That was quick," I said as he landed.

"Yes, well, I've found the very place, but you must be careful – there's lots of cars and crowds of people."

"Right guys. Hear what Jonathan says? So, keep close order, and Dixie, stay next to me. Listen for my bell. C'mon, follow Jon. We're nearly there! Last lap!"

Once again, Jonathan took to the sky, staying just above us and shouting directions, but the next few minutes were traumatic crossing a busy road – dodging cars and people. It was a nightmare! Thankfully, and not before time, Jonathan landed.

"There it is," he said and we all filed in.

"G-good heavens! What can I do for you lot?" stammered a young girl, looking astonished. Let's face it – it must have been a bit of a shock to have three dogs, a cat *and* a seagull walk into her shop.

"Well, Miss," I said. "We want a book for our Mum and something for our Dad. We've travelled all the way from Sfaka to find them Christmas gifts."

"Sfaka!" cried the girl. "I know a man from Sfaka. Comes here every year at this time and buys a certain book for his wife. Plays piano, he does."

"Plays piano?" shouted an excited Dixie. "But that's our Dad! Our Dad plays the piano!"

"Do you think it's the same man?" asked the girl.

"Well," replied Pops. "There can't be too many piano players in Sfaka, can there? Course it's the same man!"

"Right then" she said. "I know exactly what your Mum would like." And, picking out a book said, "Here you are – it's next year's diary."

I thought for a moment, looking to the others for help, as all I saw were blank pages.

"Look," said the girl. "It's hard to explain to you what it is exactly, but it's what she'd like."

"Okay," I said, "I'll go with you. How much is it?"
"Four euros," she replied.

"Four euros!" exclaimed an aghast Poppy. "Why, that's more than three tins of food!"

"Hush, Poppy," said Dixie. "We'll take it. Now, about our Dad. He loves football. Got any football books?"

"Yes," replied the girl, walking to another shelf. "See, there's one about Man U, one about Chelsea, Arsenal and…"

"What about Charlton?" I asked.

"Who?" she replied.

"Charlton! Charlton Athletic. The 'Addicks' – that's his team. He wouldn't want any of those others," I told her. "He is passionate about his Charlton."

"No, sorry" she said, searching the shelves. "Nothing on Charlton, but I've an idea. Your Dad, being a piano player, might like this novelty. Look! They're miniature pianos, and, when you turn this little handle, it plays a tune." And as she turned the handle it played 'Never On A Sunday'. "I've a few, and they each play a different tune."

"Is there one that plays something more appropriate?" asked Dixie. "Like 'We Wish You A Merry Christmas'?"

"Oh, yes," she replied. "Here you are." And, turning the handle, out came the melody.

"Excellent," I said. "That's it then. How much altogether?"

"Five euros," she replied.

"Nice one," I said. "Behind my collar you'll find a tenner. Could you take it out and put back the change? Oh, and could you please wrap the gifts up for us?"

"Yes, of course I'll wrap them. Would you like me to put little cards on and write 'to Mum and Dad'?"

"That would be very kind of you," said Dixie.

"Okay," she said, writing. "And who shall I say it's from?"

"Er, Dixie, Poppy, Alfie and Harry," I replied.

"That's only four of you. Who's the fifth?" she asked.

"That would be Jonathan, but he's not family. He's a friend," said Dixie.

"And which one of you is Jonathan?" she asked.

"I am," answered the bird. "Jonathan Livingstone Seagull."

"Jonathan Liv...!" stammered the girl. "I've got a book about you here."

"Not me," answered the bird, "but one of my ancestors. The name's been passed down for generations."

"Well, fancy that!" said the startled girl. "Jonathan Livingstone Seagull in *my* shop. Wait 'til I tell my friends!"

"That's nothing," added Pops. "Russell Crowe lives near us."

"Russell Crowe?" swooned the girl. I thought her eyes were going to pop out. "You're kidding me!"

"Yes, she is," I said, glaring at Pops. "A great joker is our Poppy. Oh! One last favour to ask. Could you tie Mum's present on my collar and Dad's to Poppy's?"

"Of course," answered the girl, and secured the gifts with brightly coloured ribbon. "There you go," she said.

"Oh, you're so kind," said Dix. "Thank you. Thank you."

Turning to look at everyone, I said, "Right, everybody ready? Time to go." Looking at the girl, I added, "We must be on our way. Thank you for your kindness and a very merry Christmas."

"And to you," said the girl, showing us out. "Go safely now. Wow! Will I remember this day!"

"What a lovely girl," said Dixie once we were outside.

"Yes, but why did you stop me telling about Russell?" asked Pops.

"Well, think about it, Pops. Once it got out that he was living in Sfaka, we'd have the whole world coming by our place to meet him. No, it's best nobody knows."

"Yeah, I guess you're right," conceded Pops.

"So," said Jon. "Let's hit the road, Jack. I'll see you safely to the outskirts and then you're on your own. Great to see you and I'll come again, maybe for a more relaxed day!"

"Thanks for everything," I said. "A Merry Christmas to you. Give our love to all our friends."

"Will do," he replied. "Let's go." And once more, he took off.

Again, we battled against the people and the cars but it was soon over and, once on the outskirts, Jonathan swooped low, soared high into the sky, did a final loop-the-loop, and was gone.

We set off at a cracking pace, happy with the way everything had gone. We made good time until we reached Pachia Ammos. We ran along the beach and I was tempted to have a dip until I was sidetracked by Dixie.

She suddenly stopped, sniffed and yelled, "This is it! This is where I was born! Can you see a large palm tree, you guys?"

"Yes, I can," replied Pops. "See fellas? Over there."

"Well," explained Dixie. "That's where I and my five brothers and sisters were born."

I had heard that story a thousand times before, but I waited patiently while she told the others all about it. Then we were off again but started to feel the strain after climbing the long hill from Kavousi to Platinos.

"Keep going, fellas. It's downhill for a while so we can catch our breath."

We loped along for about four kilometres until Poppy suddenly stopped.

"There it is!" she exclaimed.

"There it is what?" asked Alfie.

"There, by that garbage bin! The big tree! See it? That's what I was tied to for days before our Mum freed me. Our Mum cut the rope, which was attached to a chain, which was wrapped round the tree. And look! Look! The chain's still round the tree. I don't believe it!"

"If you don't stop rabbiting on, I'll put you back there," I said. "Let's get going, or else we'll still be here on Boxing Day!"

The rest of the trip was uneventful, but oh boy, were we pleased to see the house. The last hill nearly killed us – the legs wouldn't work any more.

"Thank goodness!" said Alfie. "I was beginning to think we'd never see this place again."

Just then, our Mum came out of the house, and on seeing us, cried, "Where have you been? We've been worried sick! Your Dad is out in the car looking for you. Here he comes now, and I don't think he'll be very happy with you lot!"

As Dad jumped out of the car, I thought, uh-oh! We're in for it now!

"Where've you been?" he yelled. "I've been up and down all over the place and... 'Allo? What's that tied to your collar, Harry?"

Taking hold of me, he untied the package, looked at it and said to Mum, "I do believe it's a present for you."

He grinned. "Look, it says 'To our Mum, from Dixie, Poppy, Alfie and Harry' – and look, Poppy's got something too! It says, 'To our Dad, from Dixie, Poppy, Alfie and Harry'. Wow! I can't believe it! D'you know, darling, I think they've been somewhere and bought us Christmas presents! D'you think that's possible?"

"I think anything's possible with our clever family." replied Mum. "If only they could talk."

You know, I couldn't help smiling.

Epilogue

The air was crisp with a full moon overhead. I was deep in thought, mulling over what Bobby Badger had just told me about Ike being back in town. He was a mean old bird and not to be underestimated, and as for his gang, the Clanton Brothers joining up, that made it even more scary.

Now and then a wave of panic welled up inside me. I was afraid, I must admit, afraid for all of us.

Then anger took over.

"That's it!" I thought. "Enough's enough! Time to act."

Living in this part of the world, life has been bliss and we have made many friends. Every day, a new adventure whether it be a walk in the olive groves, a romp in the hills or a swim in the sea. But most importantly, we have the greatest respect for one another. These hooligans were returning with one thought in their minds – to make our lives a misery. Well I tell you what Mr Ike, you're not about to spoil our little bit of heaven. I'm going to call a meeting with all our friends to make a plan, and you can rest assured, we'll be ready for you!